THIS JOURNAL BELONGS TO

Nicki P. Hoffman
December 1999

My twin sister, Isabel → ← Me

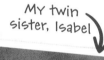

I have a new journal!

This is where I will record MY **INNERMOST** thoughts. And write song lyrics that may someday touch the hearts and souls of other people. And write lists. *(I love lists!)*

All during what might be the MOST IMPORTANT time in history: December 1999—the last month of this millennium.

Nicki!

Nicki! Come here!

Ugh. MY sister is yelling MY name. MY TWIN sister, Isabel. I'm ignoring her. She's not the boss of me.

Besides, I'M all set up here on MY purple inflatable chair with:

1. MY new journal (a gift for the last night of Hanukkah)

2. Gel pens (also new!)

3. Sour candy (the more sour, the better!)

4. Blossom, MY newly adopted companion (best Hanukkah gift ever!!!)

NICKI!!!

ARGH! Isabel woke up Blossom. I had to chase her before she got into the Cheez Balls again. (She's cute, but cleaning up puppy Cheez Ball barf is NOT FUN!)

3

Anyway, where was I? Oh Yeah.
Introducing You to MY family.

There's me, NICKI P. Hoffman, the firstborn child.

By 6 whole minutes, big deal!

Isabel! Get out of MY journal!

Me: Nicki ~~Hoffman~~ Hoffman
(don't like MY middle name)

Brown hair

Blue eyes

Favorite color: Purple

Favorite snack:
Wild Berry Pop-Tarts

Favorite TV show:
The Powerpuff Girls
(Team Blossom!)

Favorite Music: Ska,
alternative, rock. Too many
bands to count! But MY
favorite is No Doubt.

Best friend: Isabel

Her: Isabel Jane Hoffman

Blond hair

Green eyes

Favorite color: Pink

Favorite snack:
Cheez Balls

Favorite TV show:
All That

Favorite Music: Pop!
Especially Spice Girls.
She plays them A LOT.

Best friend: Me, Nicki,
of course!

You forgot Quinn, Tori, and Tiffany. They're all my best friends.

Why do you need so many friends, anyway?

Why don't you have more? And you don't like your middle name?? I think Pearl is pretty!!!

Too girly for me. And hey! You forgot to write me down as your best friend in YOUR journal!

Oops. But who's peeking at whose journal now??

You started it.

So . . . that's Isabel. We are FRATERNAL twins. Not identical.

We look a lot alike, but we have different color hair and eyes. And we are VERY different people.

Sometimes we can read each other's minds—we call it

We have the same birthday—May 22. We are GEMINI, sign of the TWINS!

More About Our Family ⭐

❤️ 😊

We celebrate both Hanukkah AND Christmas.

Mom (Robin)

- Works at a technology company
- Teaches me stuff on the computer (super fun!)
- Loves bookstores and books (so do I!)

Dad (Dave)

- Owns a coffee shop called Coffeegarden
- Teaches me about music
- Used to play guitar and sing in a grunge band (so cool!)

. . . and introducing the newest members of the Hoffman family:

MY PUPPY! BLOSSOM
I was so SURPRISED
to get her!

Isabel's kitten!
Buffy

We live in Seattle, Washington.

Seattle is AMAZING!

We're only 20 minutes from downtown by car.
You can go to Pike Place Market and buy all kinds of things, like jewelry and T-shirts and stuff. But watch out for flying fish, since the fish sellers throw fish to each other!

Our house is a short walk to Lake Washington.
And from the beach we can even see Mt. Rainier in the distance!

7

Nicki's Board Game!

Skateboard Pun! →

MY and Isabel's house! →

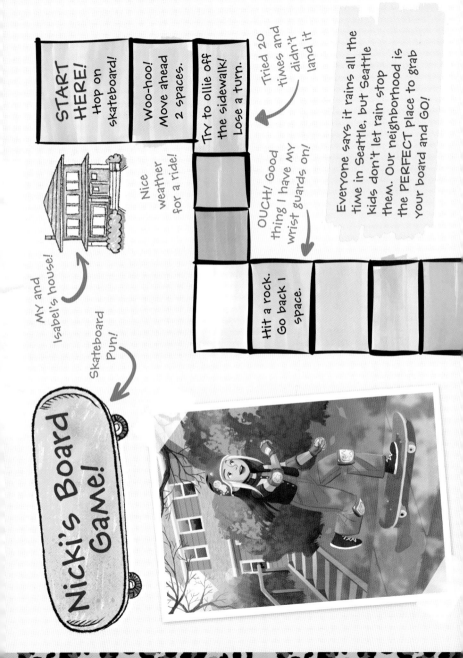

START HERE! Hop on skateboard!

Woo-hoo! Move ahead 2 spaces.

Nice weather for a ride!

Try to ollie off the sidewalk! Lose a turn.

Tried 20 times and didn't land it →

OUCH! Good thing I have MY wrist guards on! →

Hit a rock. Go back 1 space.

Everyone says it rains all the time in Seattle, but Seattle kids don't let rain stop them. Our neighborhood is the PERFECT place to grab your board and GO!

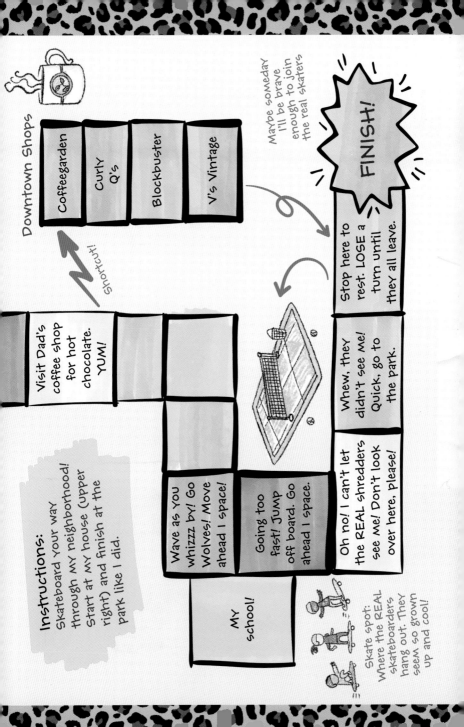

Okay, so that's not actually what I look like.

Not yet, anyway. This is the reality:

I really want to do an ollie. Dad taught me the basics of skating, but I want to learn tricks that REAL skaters do. I've tried my ollie about 3 million times, but I keep wiping out before I even get four wheels off the ground. Maybe I should stick to easy tricks, like my flippy uppy.

I usually make sure no one's around before I practice. Over the summer I went to the big skate park downtown but some older boys made fun of me when I fell down. They said, "See? Girls are bad skaters." It felt horrible. Now I don't let ANYONE see me fall.

Even if I can't do fancy tricks, I still LOVE skating! If Mom and Dad would let me, I'd ride my board everywhere. Zoom!

I was up late writing here in my journal, but Isabel started complaining about my flashlight keeping her awake. Dad came in (because Isabel is a **loudmouth** who's never heard of whispering) and told us to quiet down. So we're writing back and forth in her journal.

She can always tell when I'm worried about something because I chew on my gel pen. But what's NOT to worry about? Y2K is coming!!! Isabel thinks it's a big joke. But it's serious.

The Y2K Bug

It's a computer flaw

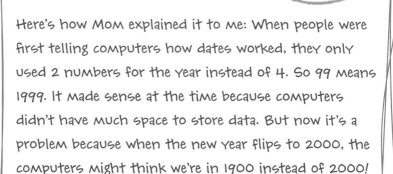

Not an insect!

Here's how Mom explained it to me: When people were first telling computers how dates worked, they only used 2 numbers for the year instead of 4. So 99 means 1999. It made sense at the time because computers didn't have much space to store data. But now it's a problem because when the new year flips to 2000, the computers might think we're in 1900 instead of 2000!

Mom says not to worry because all the computer people (including her) are working hard to fix it.

But on the news they keep saying that the government and banks and airplanes and electricity could **CRASH,** which would be a **HUGE DISASTER!**

How can we be TWINS and think so DIFFERENT??!

Me

Dizzy

Stomach hurts

Heart poundy

Weak legs

Her

La La

La

(I think I'M RIGHT and she's WRONG.)

Instead of worrying that the world might end, I'M trying to focus on the Millennium Celebration Seattle's throwing on New Year's Eve. That's something fun to look forward to.

Isabel is telling me to stop freaking out, but TALK TO THE HAND, ISABEL!!!!

OK, Isabel and I just had a great idea. We're gonna write a Y2K countdown list. (I love lists!) Maybe it will keep MY mind off the possible disasters.

COUNTDOWN LIST

10 things to do before Y2k:

1. Conquer a Fear

2. Perform an Act of Kindness

3. Get Organized

4. Do Something People Don't Think I Can Do

5. Make a New Friend

6. Dance Like It's 1999

7. Try Something New

8. Love Your Look

9. Write a Letter to Your Future Self

10. Make a Memory to Last Forever

I do twin-ky swear that I will complete the Countdown List ~~without complaining~~ to the best of my ability.

Signature _Nicki Hoffman_

HMMM... what fear should I conquer for #1? I'M afraid of...

Talking to new people

Falling off MY skateboard... especially in front of someone

Y2K

Forgetting to do MY homework

Failing a test

Dad's coffee shop losing business. What if people like the new coffee shop in town?

Someone reading MY journal

Sushi (Why am I scared of raw fish? I don't know!!)

 Time to listen to music on MY headphones until I fall asleep... bye for now.

Isabel's friends are coming.
Exciting. (NOT!)
Isabel's racing around like

I have so much to do!

I need to get ready!

And for what? Her friends since
second grade?! She's not
hosting the Queen of England.

Nicki, can I PLEASE
do your hair before
people get here?

I just shook it so it covered
my face. She is not amused.
OK, OK.

I let her put my hair up
in a high ponytail. Ow,
my scalp! But maybe now
she'll leave me alone.

ALONE

I just
thought of
a song lyric
idea!

Alone does not mean lonely ♪
Alone you can think
There's peace in the quiet . . . ♪

16

AAAAH!

Her friends are here, and they're SO LOUD. They're playing Spice Girls. Isabel is Baby Spice, as always. And she just asked ME to be Sporty Spice. Is THAT why she put my hair up like this?

NO THANK YOU! I'm not into that anymore.

I'll just sit here on MY bed with MY faithful companion, Blossom. Hey, Blossom, come back! Uh-oh. She's joining the dance. Traitor. Well, I guess SHE can be Sporty.

Uh-oh. Blossom got into the bag of Doritos 3Ds. Isabel's mad. They were for Posh Spice AKA Quinn.

I'M on a roll with these new lyrics!

No, Isabel, I don't owe you.
It's chaos in here.
I've got to GO.
Yes, Isabel, I'M leaving.

It's a good day for skateboarding anyway.

Today I met FRIENDS who SKATEBOARD! I'M SO EXCITED!

Even Isabel said,

Nicki, Your Mood ring is BLUE! It's always black or gray!!

So I told her all about MY day.

After I escaped to the park, I was trying to do a flippy uppy on MY board. But I turned it into a flippy uppy 180, which I've never done before! Some skaters saw me, including a GIRL. I NEVER see other girls skating! I'm usually super shy . . . but guess what.

I MADE FRIENDS WITH HER!

I said,

Hey, what's up?

I can't believe how brave I was.

Oh! And that means I can check off

☑ MAKE A NEW FRIEND

on MY Countdown List!!!

Ari (that's her name) is SO cool and nice and awesome.

Ari: 555-9082

18

I met her older brother, Adam, and three friends. They're SO nice—nothing like the mean boys from the skate park last summer. They're practicing tricks to show off at the Millennium Celebration, hoping to convince the city we need more skate parks. They also want to get more kids into skateboarding. And Ari said, "Especially girls."

Adam

Gregory

Shredward
(I think
that's how
you spell it??)

Crunch

We skated together, and I did something I've been afraid to do for forever. I tried my ollie and FELL in front of them! But guess what? I just got back up! And everybody cheered me on anyway!

Oh! That's another thing to cross off my Countdown List!

 CONQUER A FEAR

I'm cruising through this list! I wonder if I would be brave enough to skate in front of people at the Millennium Celebration. That might be TOO scary.

19

I still haven't even told You about the <u>zine</u> Ari Made to pass out at the Millennium Celebration.

A zine is like a homemade Magazine

Some kids are afraid to try skateboarding because they think all skateboarders are like this.

What people think skateboarders are:

Troublemakers

Rude

Only boys

Sloppy

Mean

I did Meet some Mean skaters last summer, but even they didn't act like THIS.

Her cousin who goes to college in Olympia taught her to make them. I'M taping it here so I can keep it forever!!!

But we're really:

Creative

Kind

Fun

Chill

Active

Strong

Brave

Resilient

Ari and her friends are totally like <u>this!</u>

Ari wants me to join them on New Year's Eve to skate and hand out these zines.

Zines are SO COOL. Ari's going to teach me how to make MY own!!!

Isabel is ~~SHOCKED~~ that I started the Countdown List without her. I'm like, Isabel, we're fraternal twins, not conjoined twins. She said it would be cool if we were conjoined, because then we could do everything together. I don't think so! Oh no, now Isabel's crying. Hang on.

Awww . . . Her friends don't want to dance to the Spice Girls anymore. I feel a little bad that I ditched the group. But there's no way I was going to dance onstage in front of people.

I can't stop thinking about skating at the Millennium Celebration with my new friends, though. I finally have a friend group! They make me feel strong and confident, even when I fall down.

You know what? I think I can do it!

I'M GOING TO SKATE AT THE MILLENNIUM CELEBRATION!!!

COOL

When I told Isabel, she said, "Who are you and what have you done with Nicki?" She thinks I'm too shy to skate in front of people.

Blossom believes in me, though. She wishes she could skate, too. Which reminds me—I haven't told you how I got her yet!

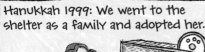

Hanukkah 1999: We went to the shelter as a family and adopted her.

SHE'S MINE AND SO CUTE!

Isabel loves cats and got a kitten she named Buffy.

Blossom doesn't love cats so much, but she and Buffy are getting used to each other.

I feed Blossom twice a day and take her outside for walks.

She doesn't go very far yet, because her legs are small, but sometimes I put her on my skateboard!

 Blossom's Bow-Wowntdown List

1. Conquer a fear: Walked past Buffy on stairs. (She pounces! She has claws!)

2. Be kind: Licked my human's face when her eyes were leaking.

3. Make a new friend: Sniffed a ~~shiwawa~~ chihuahua on the sidewalk.

4. Try something new: Instead of my bowl, drank water from the big bowl in the bathroom.

5. Make a memory: Ate SO MANY Cheez Balls!

Ari taught me how to make a zine. So . . . I made
a zine about making zines so I wouldn't forget!

Zines look weird
unfolded. But just
turn the journal
upside down and
start here on the
title page. Then
follow the pages
1, 2, 3 . . .

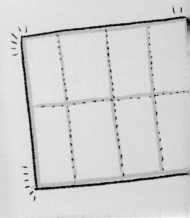

By Nicki!

HOW TO
MAKE A ZINE

A Zine about

Page 7
Now, fill your zine
with IDEAS!

Girl Power!

Page 1
Fold a piece of
paper into 8 parts.

Hot dog
style (then
unfold)

Hamburger
style (then
unfold)

Fold each
side to
meet in
the middle.

Page 2
It should look like
this unfolded:

Kind of like
a daisy with
4 petals.

Page 5
From the top, it should
look like this:

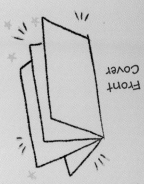

Front
Cover

Page 6
Gently fold your paper
into a book shape. It
should look like this:

Page 3
Fold the paper hamburger style again. Cut along <u>just</u> this line. Don't cut too far!

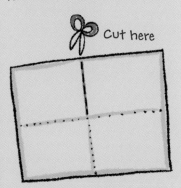

Cut here

Page 4
This is the hard part. Fold your paper hot dog style, with the part you just cut facing up. Hold both ends and push them together.

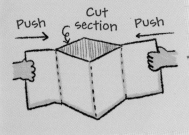

Push   Cut section   Push

Today I went to use the camcorder to film some of my tricks. Instead, I saw Isabel's video of her friends going through my side of the closet on a dare. They called it a **FREAK ZONE**

It hurt a little. But I told Isabel I don't care what anyone else thinks. I'm comfortable in what I wear. And guess what. She agreed with me! Over her friends! She said,

> Exactly! What's wrong with having your own style? Each Spice Girl does. GIRL POWER!

I was like, "Um, I'm pretty sure that girl power is more than how you dress." She said, "DUH." And I started wondering . . .

WHAT EXACTLY IS GIRL POWER?

Isabel said, "Girl power is girl power! Listen to the Spice Girls!"

Um, maybe later. (Not!)

I mean, I've heard Isabel and her friends sing Spice Girls a million times. They're always talking about girls being themselves and supporting each other. But Isabel's friends aren't supporting her AT ALL. So how DO you get girl power?

It started raining really hard, so I couldn't record my tricks anyway. (Dad said no skateboarding in the house just because I knocked over a lamp last time, and the garage is too full right now for me to skate in there.) He's on the phone, so I can't get on the Internet. And I already finished the book I was reading.

(The lampshade was barely dented!)

What should I do?

I KNOW!

ADDY LEARNS A LESSON

(Addy Learns a Lesson. GOOD BOOK!)

I just told Isabel, "I want to make a ZINE—about girl power!"

And then she and I said the EXACT same thing— we said zine-a-zine-ah!!!

TWINTUITION!

I'm starting my girl power zine research with . . .

ELISSA STEAMER
Skateboarding hero!

Elissa is my favorite character from the Tony Hawk Pro Skater game. And the only girl skater character.

She's one of only a few pro female skateboarders right now. We need more!

Elissa loved skateboarding growing up, but there weren't many women skaters. So she skated with the boys.

She won 1st place for street skating at the Slam City Jam in 1998 AND 1999. (That's a huge skateboarding competition in Canada.)

Elissa is a street skater, which means she skates on obstacles found on the street—sidewalks, ledges, and stairs. (Just like me!)

Elissa is a talented skater and brave to enter a sport that's mostly boys, which means she has tons of girl power!

Ari says you can decorate
a zine with ANYTHING.
Here are some ideas:

Candy wrapper

Tape

String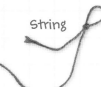

A pog (I've had this forever. No idea where it came from!)

Film negatives (Dad said I could have them)

Glitter glue

Words I wrote on the computer and printed out

This cute eraser (Ms. Bruce gave me that for getting 100% on a spelling quiz)

33 USA
1999

A stamp (this is from a postcard Grandma sent us)

gnarly

A glow-in-the-dark star that fell off the ceiling

This choker necklace (it broke in half!)

Magazine clippings (Isabel cut this out for me because it has a skateboarder)

> I can't believe it. Today when I got home I saw that ISABEL CHANGED EVERYTHING IN OUR BEDROOM!

16 days until Y2K

I got home and our whole room was covered in pink! And Isabel said:

> I updated it!

> It's today's latest trends!

> Don't you love it? I used our TWINTUITION!

That's not twintuition, Isabel. That's invasion of privacy! Invasion of <u>pinkness</u>! I made a line down the middle of our room with duct tape and stormed downstairs for some alone time.

DON'T YOU KNOW WHO I AM, ISABEL?

Time to do some research for my girl power zine! This will help take my mind off our pink bedroom.

Gwen Stefani is the lead singer of my favorite band,

NO DOUBT!

No Doubt is a ska band. That's like a regular rock band but with trombones and trumpets.

My favorite album:

Tragic Kingdom

(They released one new song this year. I'm soooo excited for the full album to come out!)

If I ever have the chance to see Gwen Stefani I have NO DOUBT I'd pee my pants
-Nicki Hoffman

Dad heard MY MUSIC blasting through MY headphones. But instead of getting mad, he started singing along!

Dad knows No Doubt ?!?

I thought Dad <u>ONLY</u> liked old-school grunge, since he used to play in a grunge band and only listens to KCMU. (That's the radio station known for playing grunge.) But Dad said, "Good music is good music" and that I should try new artists. Huh. Maybe Backstreet Boys? Ricky Martin? Destiny's Child?

But Dad and I agree:

Old-school grunge ROCKS!

(See, I listen to Isabel talk about music sometimes, plus I like to look at the lists of today's most popular music. I love lists!)

Grunge started here in Washington!

Punk + rock + metal + personal lyrics = grunge
Regular clothes (no costumes or makeup)
Anti-fame (getting famous was not the point!)

Dad's grunge band was called Sludge Confetti, and I've listened to their tapes! They rock!

I wish Dad's band hadn't broken up.

Today Isabel had a MELTDOWN at school!

I was working on my social studies homework when
Rebecca W. came back from the office and said
Isabel was freaking out in the hallway. Even though
I was still mad at her for changing our room,
I wanted to help. I ran out of
the room without even a hall
pass. I found Isabel and
hugged her. Then I told
her to breathe slowly,
like I do when I'm feeling
upset. She started to
calm down.

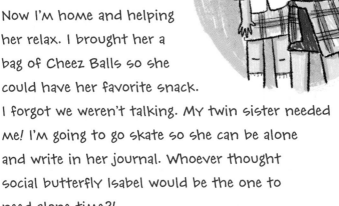

Now I'm home and helping
her relax. I brought her a
bag of Cheez Balls so she
could have her favorite snack.
I forgot we weren't talking. My twin sister needed
me! I'm going to go skate so she can be alone
and write in her journal. Whoever thought
social butterfly Isabel would be the one to
need alone time?!

I just got home

I SPRAINED MY ANKLE!!!!!!!!

Isabel and I both had bad days. A TWIN-cidence!

Ari was helping me with my ollie, which I was **SO CLOSE** to landing for the first time. But the ground was wet, and the board slipped sideways. I fell HARD, and I TOTALLY twisted my ankle. It was the worst pain ever. Then I started crying in front of everyone. I was SO EMBARRASSED.

Ari kept me calm while Shredward ran to get Dad. We had to go to the emergency room.

I got my first X-ray! I thought it would be cool to get a purple cast that my friends could sign, but the doctor said it was just a sprain. I have to wrap my ankle with a bandage, ice it, and prop it up when I'm at home. Plus, I have to be on crutches for ONE WHOLE WEEK!

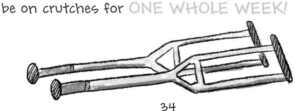

Just when I was getting good enough to skate at the Millennium Celebration. I feel like I'm letting my new friends down. Now I can't practice my skating! I was supposed to show girls that they can be skaters too! So much for girl power. I'm letting everyone down.

I feel like such a

FAILURE

Hoffman, Nicki P.
DOB: 05/22/90
MRN: 439526
Liu, Rebecca M.D.

To cheer us both up, Isabel helped me look through magazines to find MY unique style. (I guess I'm still a little hurt by the whole "freak zone" thing.) And it was actually fun!

I love purple!

GIRL POWER

Look at this jacket! SO COOL!

I've always wanted to color MY hair a bright color. I wonder . . .

I asked Isabel if she thought I'd look good with purple streaks. And she said:

YESSSSS!!!!

Awesome

I don't know if Mom and Dad will let me dye MY hair again, though.

Mom and Dad said YES!!! I can only use washable color. But I still can't believe it!!!

Isabel brushed the color onto my hair.

We took a style quiz from one of Isabel's magazines while it dried.

Isabel gave me the CUTEST space buns!

I LOVE IT!!!!

LOVE YOUR LOOK

Hey Isabel, thanks for helping me with my hair.
I love it.

You're welcome! It was fun helping
you figure out your style.

What did that quiz say my style was again?

mysterious moon. And I got shooting
star. Because I'm sparkly, I guess!

Hmmm . . . maybe our bedroom DOES
need a style update. Except one that's
Mysterious Moon AND Shooting Star.

ARE YOU SERIOUS?!?!
YES YES YES
TIMES A MILLION!

Whoa. Slow down. One condition.

Anything!

I get to help you organize your side.

What's wrong with my side?!?
I know where everything is.

I just found your Spiceworld CD in the closet
with a Fruit Roll-up stuck to it.

OK, maybe I could use a little help . . .

~~Bossing Isabel around~~ Helping Isabel get organized was . . . fun!

I don't think this counts for getting organized for MY Y2K list, since it's not MY space. But I'll think of something else to do . . .

It takes me three times as long to do everything on crutches. My classroom is on the second floor. The hall aide told me to use the elevator. We have an elevator?

There was a fifth-grader in there already. She said, "Hi, I'm Jessica." She uses a wheelchair—with butterfly clips on the spokes!

That elevator moves s-l-o-w, so we had time to talk. Jessica is really smiley, so I forgot about being nervous around new people and told her how I wiped out on my board and sprained my ankle.

And guess what. She told me she does tricks too, but in her wheelchair! And she did a wheelie! Right there in the elevator!

Then I had a **BRILLIANT** thought.

I said,

You should come to the skate spot to practice!

That sounds awesome!

she said back.

When we got off the elevator, Jessica wrote her phone number on MY Trapper Keeper. I can't believe I made **ANOTHER** friend! Too bad I can't check Make a New Friend off MY countdown list twice. There's no way I'M going to finish it before the new millennium!

P.S. Before I crutched away, Jessica said,

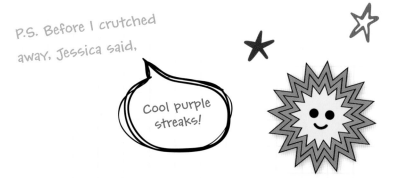

Cool purple streaks!

It's Christmas Eve!!!

Did I mention our family celebrates Hanukkah AND Christmas? Well, we do. And earlier tonight carolers came to the door, and Isabel said,

> It's Kat! With her brother Jack and their grandma Virginia!

And that's when I finally got to meet my twin's new friends! Kat is Isabel's new friend who loves fashion and crafts. Virginia owns V's Vintage, and she brought an old wagon for me to ride in! At first I was a little embarrassed to get pulled around, but singing carols was so fun I didn't mind. Dad opened Coffeegarden just for us, and we drank hot chocolate. YUM!

When we got home, Mom, Dad, Isabel, and I put out some of Mom's sugar cookie blossoms for Santa (and ate some, of course).

Isabel and I have been sleeping downstairs so I don't have to struggle up the steps. It's like a big sleepover!

HAPPY HOLIDAYS

Time to sleep. ZZZZ.

MERRY CHRISTMAS, JOURNAL!!

Kat and Isabel made these from bandannas. Isabel has gotten so crafty!

Ugly wallpaper border is GONE

New lavender walls! (MY favorite color, but pastel like Isabel likes!)

Even Isabel was surprised by this Yin-Yang rug Mom got at V's Vintage!

I got the **BIGGEST** surprise! Isabel dragged me upstairs and shouted, "Room Reveal!" I couldn't believe it. Our room had been TRANSFORMED! (Isabel told me that's the REAL reason we've been sleeping downstairs.) **IT'S PERFECT!**

Best pillow ever!

Finally, a place to put all my grin pins

New comforters! So cool!

Isabel gets me now. This room is perfect.

Mom took today off so we could have a fun family trip to downtown Seattle!

First we walked around Pike Place Market. (It took longer than usual with MY crutches.) The fish stands were **VERY** stinky, as usual. But we got to see a fish fly through the air, which was so cool! Then, for the first time, Mom and Dad let us each stick a piece of gum on the wall at this theater they like, where there's a

GUM WALL.

Gross! (But fun!)

Pike Place Market

Then we went to M. Coy Books, because Mom LOVES bookstores. (Well, we all do.) There were books tucked into every tiny corner. And guess what I found. Zines!!! Dad helped me pick one out about music. It gave me so many ideas for MY girl power zine!

Next we went to the Space Needle so Isabel could conquer her fear of heights. It was so cool to go up to the observation deck and see ALLLLL of Seattle. But it made me sad, too. Right below us is where my friends are going to do tricks and pass out zines in a few days. But even if I'm off my crutches, there's no way I'll be healed enough to skate.

WOW!

We went to Maneki for dinner. I've been nervous to try sushi but wanted to check off another countdown challenge. I ordered a smoked salmon roll. And guess what. I liked it! It did NOT smell like the Pike Place fish stands.

TRY SOMETHING NEW

It was an AMAZING day! And we'll be back in just a few days for the Millennium Celebration. Even though I can't skate, I can't wait to cheer on my friends.

amazing

Now to work on my girl power zine! (One good thing about not being able to skate is that I have lots more time for zine-making.)

I **FINALLY** don't have to use crutches, so I took Blossom down to the skate spot to hang out. (I'm not allowed on MY board yet, though.)

Jessica came too! She showed off her wheelie and tried out the slope we use as a ramp. So awesome.

Shredward is learning to noseslide the ledge. Ari teased him by showing off her crooked grind, which is even harder. They're going to be so good skating at the Millennium Celebration!

Blossom also showed off HER tricks!

I told Ari and Jessica that I'M still upset about spraining MY ankle. Jessica reminded Me that an injury isn't the end of the world and that I'm almost done with MY recovery. And Ari said that being able to skateboard isn't the only cool thing about Me, and injuries are just part of skateboarding. I felt a little better.

They've decided that Coffeegarden is THE place to hang out after skating. While we were there, I showed them both some of MY girl power zine. They loved it! Ari said it was cool that I was doing something so creative while I'm injured. They both asked for copies, but I'M not sure it's good enough to be a **REAL** zine.

Oh! I almost forgot to say that Isabel was at Coffeegarden, too. She was AWESOME and totally stood up for herself against this girl who was being mean named CaMMy. GIRL POWER! I gave Isabel a twin-ky link high five.

Today I was finally allowed to skateboard again, so I was **EXCITED!** But when I got to the skate spot, my friends were talking, not skating! They said the Millennium Celebration was canceled because the city thought something bad might happen.

My mind froze. Ari asked if I was okay. No, I thought. I am not okay. I KNEW Y2K was going to be bad and scary!

I found Isabel at the tennis courts (when did she get kind of good at tennis?) and told her the news. We ran all the way home, even though it hurt my ankle a little.

Mom and Dad had already heard the news, and they gave us a big hug. My Y2K worries were spinning out of control again.

But Dad said,

The city is just being extra careful, so DON'T WORRY.

And Mom said,

We're working hard on Y2K, so DON'T WORRY.

And Isabel said,

We'll find a way to celebrate the new millennium, so DON'T WORRY.

It's not so easy to stop worrying. But Isabel is right. We should still celebrate . . . somehow.

After some thinking, we both had the same idea:
We'll throw a New Year's Eve party at Coffeegarden!

TWINTUITION!

Isabel was like,

We'll need this!

What about this?

Fabric and papers and gel pens were flying! It was a party-planning tornado! I remembered the Countdown List—Get Organized. I said "Isabel, please pause." Then I ORGANIZED our party ideas into a list and typed it up for both of us. (I ♡ LISTS!)

GET ORGANIZED

Dad said it was just the push he needed to refresh Coffeegarden!

Y2K Party Tasks

Creative direction	Isabel
Organizing and scheduling	Nicki
Making invitations	Nicki
Passing out invitations	Nicki and skateboard friends
Party space	Dad
Decorations + supplies	Isabel, Virginia, and Kat
Music	Everyone adds ideas, Nicki organizes
Wardrobe	Isabel
Menu	Isabel
Desserts	Mom
Party favors	Isabel, Virginia, and Kat
Book drive donations	Everyone!

We're going to check off Perform an Act of Kindness with a BOOK DRIVE!

PERFORM AN ACT OF KINDNESS

I made a flyer to invite people. It was fun!! I skated to the library and made <u>LOTS OF COPIES</u>. The librarian said she loved how we were donating books.

Ari and the other skaters are going to help me pass out flyers to the whole neighborhood.

And don't tell Isabel, but . . . I also made some copies of my girl power zine. I don't know if I'm ready to share it. But I have them just in case. Shhh!!!

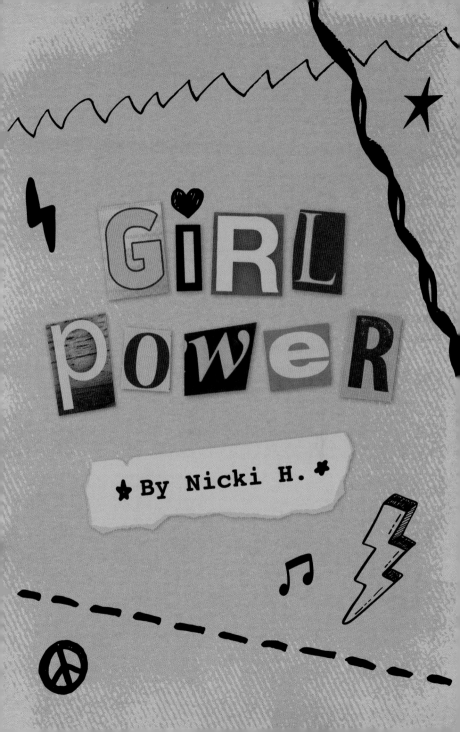

Girl power means that
girls are . . .

STRONG

unique

kind

Brave

Funny

Smart

CONFIDENT

Girls
rule!

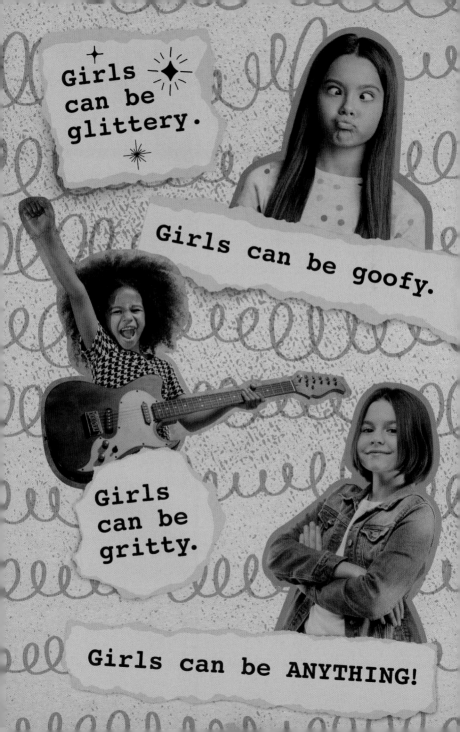

Girls can be glittery.

Girls can be goofy.

Girls can be gritty.

Girls can be ANYTHING!

Girl Power Heroes
(Just a few!)

⚡SERENA WILLIAMS⚡

won her first US Open at age 17.

Sister power! Serena and her big sister Venus have CHANGED THE GAME of tennis.

FOCUSED **HARDWORKING**

UNSTOPPABLE

STRONG

LITTLE SISTER WINS BIG

By Mel Hammond

Seventeen-year-old Serena Williams stunned the US Open crowd Saturday after defeating top-ranked player Martina Hingis. She is the first African American woman in 41 years to win the national title.

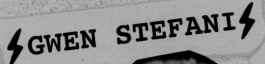 **GWEN STEFANI**

is transforming
music with her
ska band
No Doubt!

She has . . .

unique
STYLE

a special
SOUND

powerful
LYRICS

 ELISSA STEAMER

One of the first-
ever women
skaters to go pro
(for Toy Machine
Skateboards).

Featured in two
skateboarding
videos!

WHAT does

GIRL PWR

mean

to YOU ?

Look at the flyer I made for the party!

Community Celebration for the

NEW MiLLeNNium

Friday, December 31, 1999, 7PM COFFEEGARDEN

Performances, music, food, drinks, time capsule, and more!

FREE ADMISSION
with a book donation!

No book = $5 donation to Seattle Children's Hospital for cover charge

TOMORROW IS THE DAY!

The day that I've been worrying about. Been thinking
about. Been getting ready for . . . our millennium
party! New Year's Eve! Y2K! The last day before
everything might change . . . and Isabel is yelling
to me:

> Okay Nicki, we get
> it! Come help finish
> these decorations!

We've been working SO HARD on the party.
And we helped Dad turn Coffeegarden into the
COOLEST coffee shop in town! So I really hope
the world doesn't end on Y2K so we can enjoy the
new Coffeegarden and all the other things that have
changed. I never imagined I'd adopt a puppy and
make skater friends and learn tricks and sprain my
ankle and eat sushi and get a
cool new room and figure
out my style.

I even let Isabel put
an outfit together
for me for the party!
She gets me now.

Time for bed.

But I can't sleep. Too nervous. Isabel's awake, too.

Oh no, what is she doing?

The party was AMAZING!!!

EVERYONE came! My friends, Isabel's new friends, Isabel's old friends (who said "sorry" to Isabel . . . and then to me for mocking my style!), and so many people from the neighborhood we didn't know but now we do. There were even surprises:

Surprise #1: The mayor showed up! He came to thank us for the book drive. We got PILES and PILES of books to donate to the children's hospital where they took care of my ankle!

Surprise #2: Dad rocked out on his guitar—and he performed my original lyrics set to his music! My words! Being heard—by everyone (gulp). And they all loved it!

Surprise #3: I handed out my zine! What?! YUP! I even went up to the mic and read from it! I guess I didn't have to skate at the Millennium Celebration to spread girl power after all.

DO SOMETHING
PEOPLE DON'T
THINK I CAN DO ☑

It was so cool to hear one of MY songs performed, but it was **SUPER** cool to see Dad play guitar like he used to.

Dad sang MY lyrics!!!!

After the midnight countdown, Mom heard from her work—the computers were OKAY! Y2OK!

I'M SO HAPPY!!! THE PARTY WAS SO FUN!

Here's MY letter I wrote for the time capsule tonight!

(I printed it so I could save a copy for you, Journal.)

Dear Future Me:

If you're reading this, that means **Y2K** didn't crash the world!

In **1999**, I was 9 years old. In the *new millennium*, I will turn **double digits!** So will my twin. Will that make us **quadruple digits?**

I hope I will land more **gnarly** tricks on my skateboard! And write *lots* of songs and make *lots* of **ZINES!** Maybe I'll even have my own guitar! No matter what happens, I'll be okay because I have my mom and dad and Blossom and Buffy and my **twin** sister **Isabel!**

Sincerely,

Nicki Pearl Spice, Seattle Washington

Dad said MY middle name always reminds him of the band Pearl Jam, so NOW I like it!

WRITE A LETTER TO YOUR FUTURE SELF

Now that we're home, Isabel and I can't stop talking about the party, even though it's WAYYYYYY past our bedtime.

Twin win! I told Isabel.

Twin win! Isabel told me.

No matter what happens, the new millennium will be amazing because we'll be together! Good night, Journal!

10, 9, 8, 7, 6, 5, 4, 3, 2 . . . Y2K!

MAKE A MEMORY TO LAST FOREVER

COUNTDOWN LIST

10 things I did before Y2K!!!

1. Conquer a Fear ☑ tried a trick and fell in front of people

2. Perform an Act of Kindness ☑ book drive

3. Get Organized ☑ party planning checklist

4. Do Something People Don't Think I Can Do ☑ shared MY zine!

5. Make a New Friend ☑ Ari, Jessica, Adam, Gregory, Crunch, and Shredward!

6. Dance Like It's 1999 ☑ with Isabel in the bedroom

7. Try Something New ☑ ate sushi

8. Love Your Look ☑ colored MY hair purple!

9. Write a Letter to Your Future Self ☑ put a copy in a time capsule

10. Make a Memory to Last Forever ☑ millennium party!!

Nicki Hoffman
Ms. Bruce
Grade 4

10 Girl Power Moments of the 1990s

1. 1991 – Zines by and for girls and women grew.

1991 was when girls in the punk music scene really started using zines as a way to express themselves. People make zines about almost ANYTHING, but a lot of girls started using zines in the early 1990s to write about girl power and feminism. They also used their zines to make sure girls had a place in everything from skateboarding to science.

2. 1991 – The first website in the US came online.

While scientists in Europe invented the World Wide Web (www) in 1989, it wasn't until 1991 that the United States had its first website. That year, scientific librarian Louise Addis helped create a website that made information available to physicists all around the world. It was the world's first online library!

These kids are using the Internet for schoolwork, just like I do!

3. 1991 – US women's national soccer team wins first Women's World Cup.

The US women's national soccer team was responsible for soccer getting cooler throughout the 1990s, especially to girls. The very first Women's World Cup was in 1991, and the US team won that. They also won gold at the first summer Olympic games where women's soccer was included, in 1996. And then earlier this year, in July, the US team won the Women's World Cup AGAIN! Mia Hamm is one of the big stars of the team, and she holds the record for most international goals scored.

Mia Hamm is a fierce competitor at soccer!

4. 1992 – Dr. Mae Jemison becomes the first African American woman in space.

Mae Jemison is a doctor, engineer, and astronaut, which is impressive enough—and then she went to space! She always knew she liked science, and seeing Lieutenant Uhura (played by African American actress Nichelle Nichols) on *Star Trek* growing up made her want to travel to space. She made 127 orbits around Earth before coming home. She also appeared on *Star Trek: The Next Generation* in 1993, so she's a real astronaut and a TV astronaut!

Look how cool she is, floating in space!

5. 1996 – Madeleine Albright is the United States' first woman secretary of state.

Madeleine Albright was born in Prague, in what is now the Czech Republic. She and her family moved to the United States when it wasn't safe for them in their home country anymore. Then she became a US citizen while in college and began working in a bunch of different government roles. President Clinton first made her the ambassador to the United Nations and then appointed her secretary of state.

Madeleine Albright takes her work super seriously, because it's so important.

6. 1996 – *Matilda* the movie comes out.

In 1996, the movie *Matilda* came out, and it's one of my favorite books and movies EVER. *Matilda* the book was written by Roald Dahl, and in the movie Matilda is played by Mara Wilson. Matilda is a girl who has a mean family and principal, reads a lot, and has the power to move things with her mind. Matilda uses her powers and voice to defend herself and others. I really admire other girls who use their power for good and to help people.

7. 1997 – Lilith Fair music tour starts.

Here's Sarah McLachlan performing at Lilith Fair, which she created.

The 1990s have been an awesome time for music by women and girls, and Lilith Fair was a big part of that. Lilith Fair is a traveling concert FULL of women singers and musicians created by the singer Sarah McLachlan. She was frustrated that women musicians were not being treated as well as men, so she wanted to help uplift other women in music. They even donated money to charity from doing these concerts.

8. 1997 – *Secret Paths in the Forest* is released.

The 1990s have been an excellent decade for video games, with some important games coming out for girls and women. One game I like is *Secret Paths in the Forest*, which was created by a woman named Brenda Laurel for her company Purple Moon, because she really wanted to make games for girls. For a long time, people thought only boys could like video games, but my whole family plays PlayStation and computer games, and three of us are girls. My mom likes that my sister and I want to learn about technology.

Here's Brenda Laurel with girls showing how excited they are about Purple Moon games!

9. 1998 – *The Powerpuff Girls* starts airing on TV.

My favorite Powerpuff Girl is Blossom, because she's really smart and a good leader. Plus, she bosses her sisters around, which is hard to do—take it from me! The Powerpuff Girls show that you shouldn't judge a book by its cover, and that even young girls can be powerful and make change. There are SO MANY cartoons right now showing that there are lots of ways to be a girl and that we can have lots of different interests and personality types. My mom says this is new for television, and I love it!

10. 1998 – Snowboarding is at the Olympics for the first time—with CB Burnside.

I loved watching Cara-Beth (CB) Burnside compete in Nagano, Japan. She had already won first place in the Winter X Games half pipe competition and then took fourth place in the Olympics half pipe snowboarding that same year! AWESOME! CB is a great skateboarder too. She was the first woman with a signature skate shoe with her sponsor Vans and the first woman on the cover of *Thrasher*, the skateboard magazine.

CB Burnside looks so cool snowboarding!

I couldn't have made this journal without the help of

Jennifer Roy

This is Jennifer when she was 9 like me

And this is her twin, Julia

Jennifer is six minutes older than her twin sister, and one inch shorter—just like me! Also like me, she loves music, including grunge and No Doubt, and when she was nine, she had a skateboard that she rode all over her neighborhood.

Jennifer and her twin, Julia DeVillers, are also writing a hardcover book about our adventures!

You get both sides of the story!

ISABEL AND NICKI: Countdown to Y2K

Jennifer and Julia wrote it together! (With my and Isabel's help, of course.)

You're going to love it!!!